P9-ELQ-286

BAD KITTY

Puppy's BIG DAY

NICK BRUEL

SQUARE FISH

A NEAL PORTER BOOK
ROARING BROOK PRESS
New York

For George and Siobhan: friends and family

An Imprint of Macmillan
175 Fifth Avenue
New York, NY 10010
mackids.com

BAD KITTY: PUPPY'S BIG DAY. Copyright © 2015 by Nick Bruel.
All rights reserved. Printed in the United States of America by
LSC Communications, Harrisonburg, Virginia.

Square Fish and the Square Fish logo are trademarks of Macmillan and
are used by Roaring Brook Press under license from Macmillan.

Our books may be purchased in bulk for promotional, educational, or business use.
Please contact your local bookseller or the Macmillan Corporate and Premium
Sales Department at (800) 221-7945 ext. 5442 or by e-mail at
MacmillanSpecialMarkets@macmillan.com.

Library of Congress Cataloging-in-Publication Data

Bruel, Nick, author, illustrator.
Bad Kitty : Puppy's Big Day / Nick Bruel.
p. cm
"A Neal Porter Book."
Summary: Uncle Murray takes Puppy on a walk on a day that Bad Kitty is being unusually difficult, but has several unpleasant encounters with a police officer and one mean dog along the way. Text is interspersed with information about dog behavior, pet care, and more.
ISBN 978-1-250-07330-3 (paperback)
[1. Dogs—Fiction. 2. Cats—Fiction. 3. Humorous Stories.] I. Title.
PZ7.B82832Badp 2015
[E]—dc23

2014010357

Special Book Fair Edition ISBN 978-1-62672-307-8
Originally published in the United States by Roaring Brook Press
First Square Fish Edition: 2016
Square Fish logo designed by Filomena Tuosto

3 5 7 9 10 8 6 4

AR: 1.0 / LEXILE: 500L

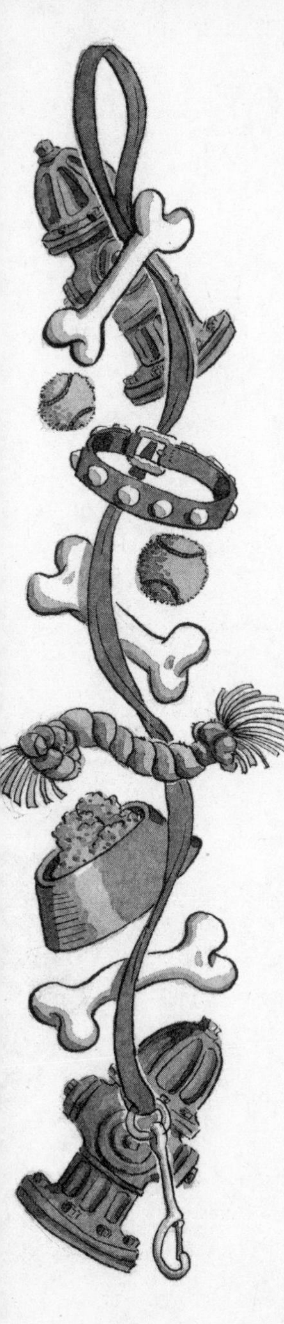

• CONTENTS •

• PART ONE •

PUPPY LAW

In case it's not obvious, Kitty is in a very, very,

VERY

bad mood today.

And nobody knows why.

It's worse than the day someone said Kitty needed a bath.

THE DAILY NOOZ

ALL THE NEWS THAT WILL FIT ON PAPER

RAMPAGE

The National Guard was called in yesterday after a local cat refused to take a bath.
... seen such ...

It's worse than the day they discontinued her favorite brand of cat litter.

THE DAILY NOOZ

WE MAKE THE NEWS SO YOU DON'T HAVE TO

HORROR

Hundreds fled from a local shopping mall today after a local ...
went ...

It's worse than the day they canceled her favorite TV show *Claw and Order*.

THE DAILY NOOZ

MMMM, MMMM . . . NOW THAT'S GOOD NEWS

HORRIBLE RAMPAGE

Hostages were finally released today following a 5-hour stand off that took place after a local cat lost its mind

Police were

It's even worse than the day we brought Puppy home.

THE DAILY NOOZ

NEWS, NEWS, IT'S GOOD FOR YOUR HEART. THE MORE YOU READ, THE MORE YOU . . .

RAMPAGING HORROR

What is it with this cat?! Just about every month it has some sort of complete melt- that sends every fleeing

Speaking of Puppy, here he comes now!

Oh, boy. Puppy, if I were you, I'd leave Kitty alone today. I don't think she's in the mood to play with you. Honestly, I don't think she's EVER in the mood to play with you. But today it'll be like playing with a lit firecracker.

Oh, Puppy. Sometimes you just need to listen to reason.

Too late.

HANG ON, PUPPY! I'M CALLING FOR HELP!

15 MINUTES LATER . . .
UNCLE MURRAY IS HERE! I got here as fast as I could! What's the emergency? Are you trying to give that goofy cat a b—?

DON'T SAY IT! DON'T EVEN SAY THE WORD!

We don't know why Kitty is in such a foul mood. But we really need you to take Puppy out of the house while we either sort this out or move into a new house.

Awww! What's the matter, ya goofy kitty cat? Are you a grumpy little pussycat? Who's a crabby little kitty? I think you are! Yes, you are! I think you're a crabby, wabby little pussy . . .

AIEEE

EEE!
The Big Book of ROBOTS

WHOA! That was intense! We were lucky to get out of there alive, pooch! Sometimes I'm not convinced she really is a cat. I'm thinking she's more like a weird cross between an electric eel and a howler monkey.

But never mind all that. This ought to be fun! It's been a while since I spent time with a dog. You wanna go to the movies? Or maybe a ball game? Do you know how to play checkers? Maybe we could . . .

HEY YOU!

Ummm . . . Hello, officer.
Good morning to you.
Is there anything I
can do for you?

YOU GOT A LEASH FOR THAT DOG?

Well, uh, no, officer. Actually, I don't. We were in an awful hurry to leave the house just now, you see, and I guess we forgot it. It's a funny story, actually, if you'd like to hear it. See, there's this goofy cat, and sometimes I'm not even sure if she is a cat. As I was just saying to my dog friend here, sometimes I think . . . and you'll think this is funny . . . sometimes I think she's really a cross between an electric . . .

YOU NEED A LEASH FOR THAT DOG! IT'S THE LAW! I'M GIVING YOU A TICKET! THE NEXT TIME I SEE YOU, THERE BETTER BE A LEASH ON THAT DOG! YA GET ME?!
Yes, officer. Thank you, officer.

Well, I for one am NOT going back into that house! Maybe I'll just use my belt here for the time being.

Come on, pooch. Quit your fidgeting! I'm tryin'to get this belt on ya before I get into more trouble.

Say, what ya got there?

EWWW! YUCK! GROSS! THAT'S DISGUSTING!
SICK! GET RID OF THAT THING! HACK! IS IT ALIVE?! ICK! BLECH!

Oh, wait. It's just a toy. But it's still pretty gross. I'll just toss it into the first garbage can we . . .

WHINE
WHINE
WHINE
WHINE
WHINE
OKAY! OKAY! You can keep it! YEESH! But YOU have to carry it, not ME!

Hey! Wait a minute!
Where'd ya go?

Oh, there you are, pooch!
WHEW! You had me worried.
I thought I'd lost ya there
for a second.

WAIT! WHAT ARE YOU
DOING? NO! DON'T! STOP
THAT RIGHT NOW!
STOP THAT BEFORE . . .

HEY, YOU!!

Too late.

SCRATCH
SCRATCH

Hello again, officer. Lovely day today, isn't it?
YOU GONNA CLEAN UP AFTER THAT DOG?!

Well, officer, do you remember earlier how I was telling you about how I had to leave the house in a big hurry? You remember that, don't you? It was all because of this cat. She can be quite fierce. Really! Anyway, to make a long story short, I left the house so fast that I forgot the leash AND a bag. Silly me! Ordinarily, I would never forget such things. See, I'm quite the advocate of both canine law and sanitation. Why, just the other day my wife was saying to me, "Murray, you should have been a policeman . . .

YA GOTTA CLEAN UP AFTER THAT DOG! IT'S THE LAW! HERE'S A BAG AND ANOTHER TICKET!
Thank you, officer.

HOLY SALAMI! This whole dog-walking thing is starting to cost me some big bucks!

C'mon, pooch. Let's get to the park before I get into any more trouble.

10 MINUTES LATER . . .
Ahhhh! Much better! The sun. The grass. The fresh air. Life is good at the park. This is where you can just let go of all your worries.
OGS
WED

HEY, YOU! CAN'T YOU READ?!
Now, this is starting to get just plain ridiculous!
NO DOGS ALLOWED

Are you talking to me, officer?
NO! I'M TALKING TO THE DOG!

The dog can't read, officer.
WHAT ARE YOU? SOME KIND OF WISE GUY?

NO! NO, OFFICER! I meant no disrespect!
WELL... I'LL LET YOU OFF THIS TIME.

Oh, thank you, officer! Thank you! Thank you!
UNLESS...

Unless what, officer?
UNLESS YOUR DOG DOESN'T HAVE A LICENSE! DOES YOUR DOG HAVE A LICENSE?!

But . . . uh . . . but . . .
The dog doesn't drive.

YOU *ARE* A WISE GUY! HERE'S YOUR TICKET, WISE GUY! NOW GET THAT DOG A LICENSE AND TAKE HIM TO A DOG PARK WHERE OTHER DOGS ARE, WISE GUY!

NO DOGS ALLOWED

THAT TEARS IT!
YAWN

The time has come for someone to stand up for dogs' rights in this country! The time has come to reform a system that tickets innocent dog walkers! The time has come to unite all dogs and their walkers and fight the powers that push us down! Someone needs to represent the basic rights and freedoms of all canines and canine perambulators!

I AM THAT SOMEONE! FOR I AM

UNCLE MURRAY—

KA-
FLOP

HEY, YOU!
Hello, officer.
Fine day, isn't it?

KITTY'S HORRIBLE BUT TRUE FACTS ABOUT DOGS
Why Do Dogs Need To Be Walked?

This is poop. 

This is a time bomb. 

Now imagine if some maniac invented a time bomb filled with poop and pee. Someone did. This monstrous combination is known as a dog.

The only way to diffuse this poop bomb from exploding all over your nice clean home and destroying everything you hold dear is by taking it for a walk.

This is not the case for cats.

Cats are delicate, tidy creatures who perform their elimination under controlled conditions. Meaning, they do their business in a litter box out of view.

But not dogs. Dogs need to be walked at least twice a day so that they can relieve themselves anywhere and everywhere they want regardless of the weather outside. It could be raining baseball bats and you'll STILL have to take that dog outside for the privilege of picking up his droppings with a bag. Lucky you.

This is even worse with puppies who need to pee about every 4 hours. That means you'll be walking him 6 times a day or more unless you want to see your stamp collection float away in a river of urine.

Plus, to make things worse, dogs need those walks for exercise because they don't have the insight to sleep 20 hours a day like cats. Most veterinarians say the average dog should be outside for at least 2 hours a day. Good luck with THAT.

• PART TWO •

PUPPY LOVE

And it looks like you've already made a new little friend!
SNIFF

Let's see now . . . You had grilled chicken with herbed garden vegetables dog food this morning. Very nice.

You had garlic roasted beef liver for dinner last night But you didn't like that as much. Understandable. Understandable.

Ah, but you managed to steal some scraps of Chinese food takeout last night as well. Shrimp chow fun, I believe. Clever boy!

Your garden grows tulips in the spring and Russian sage . . . no . . . sorry, sorry . . . Mexican sage in the fall.

You live in a three-bedroom ranch style home with a backyard and a porch and a very ornery cat—sorry about that.

No serious allergies. Your blood pressure is normal. You're due for a distemper booster shot. Your favorite color is yellow. You like sunsets, jazz, and long walks in the park. And you're a Capricorn.

YOU'RE A CAPRICORN! I'M A TAURUS! That means we're compatible!

HUBBA HUBBA!

HELLOOOOO, GOOD LOOKIN'

ROOTY TOOTY– YOU'RE A CUTIE!

HEY, ANGEL! WHAT HAPPENED TO YOUR WINGS?

Awwwwww!
Now isn't that just adorable?
WOOF ARF
BARK ARF
HUBBA WOOF

So, handsome . . . Now that you and I are boyfriend and girlfriend, I think that you need to give me a lovely little present! Boyfriends always give their girlfriends lovely little presents—beautiful, charming, lovely little presents to express their undying love.

Oh, my stars! A lovely little stuffed mouse toy! FOR ME?! What a lovely surprise! Oh, you shouldn't have, you incurable romantic, you!

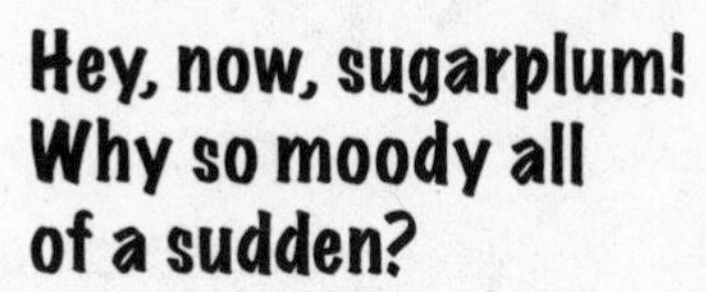
Hey, now, sugarplum!
Why so moody all
of a sudden?

GRRRRRRRRRRRRRRRR

BARK BARK BARK
BARK BARK BARK
BARK BARK BARK

BARK BARK BARK
BARK BARK BARK
BARK BARK
HOLY SALAMI! He's stronger than he looks!
We can work this out! What we have is special!

YEOWTCH!
SNAP!
BARK
BARK
BARK
BARK
Our love can never die! We owe it to our future grandchildren!

STOP IT! CUT IT OUT!
STOP THAT RIGHT NOW!
BARK
BARK
BARK
BARK
BARK
BARK
We can go into couples counseling!

NO! BAD PUPPY! BAD, BAD PUPPY! I'M SURPRISED AT YOU! BAD PUPPY! BAD!
WHINE
HEY! That's my boyfriend you're yelling at! Get your hands off of him!

Of course . . . uh . . . I could be wrong. I could be overreacting. I mean, who am I to judge the actions of man's best friend. One could easily make the argument that I . . . that I . . . I . . . I . . .
GRRRRRR

AIEE
WOOF
WOOF
WOOF

EEEEEEEEEEE
BARK
BARK
BARK

EEEEK!
WOOF WOOF WOOF
BARK BARK BARK

GO AWAY! SHOO! BAD DOGGIES!
SCRAM! VAMOOSE! GET OUTTA HERE!
WOOF
BARK
WOOF
BARK
WOOF
BARK

I think they're starting to quiet down.
WOOF BARK WOOF BARK YIPES YIPES

Now I don't hear anything. Maybe they've finally calmed down.

All right, ya goofy pooches! I'm sending one of my feet down! I don't want any biting or gnawing or chewing of any sort! Do you hear me?

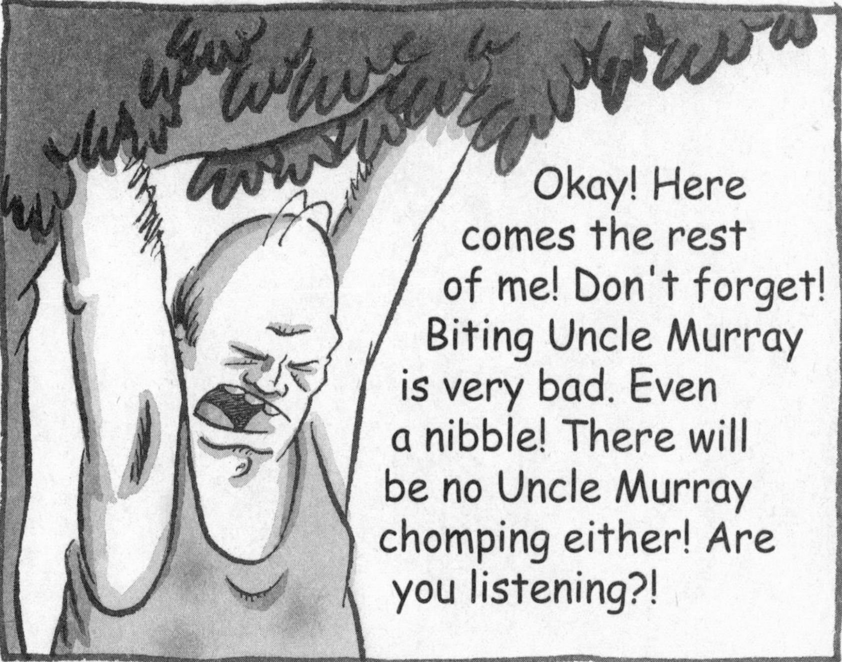
Okay! Here comes the rest of me! Don't forget! Biting Uncle Murray is very bad. Even a nibble! There will be no Uncle Murray chomping either! Are you listening?!

Uh-oh.

KITTY'S HORRIBLE BUT TRUE FACTS ABOUT DOGS

Why Do Dogs Sniff Butts?

Dogs smell. There are two ways to interpret that sentence. And they're both right.

1. Dogs are smelly. The odor of a wet dog will make you want to rip the nose off your face just to distract you from the pain.

2. Dogs know how to smell. One-third of a dog's brain is dedicated to interpreting smells. (Apparently, the other two-thirds are dedicated to drooling and pooping, but that's a topic for another time.) This means that dogs sense the world around them even more with their noses than they do with their eyes or ears.

A dog's butt gives off a strong odor from an anal gland inside it that can give other dogs a lot of information about it—like what it recently ate, how healthy it is, and even its mood.

So when a dog meets another dog, do they say "Hello. How are you?" No. They can't talk. Do they shake hands? No. They don't have hands. Do they exchange business cards? No. They can't read. Instead, the best way dogs get to know each other is by sniffing each other's butts. Horrible, but true.

Cats, on the other hand, never conduct such behavior. Cats greet each other by licking each other's whiskers, shaking tails, and handing each other formal, handwritten invitations to visit their litter boxes at the earliest convenient opportunity.

Editor's Note: Cats sniff each other's butts, too. They just don't like to talk about it.

• PART THREE •

PUPPY LOST

I can't believe that I barked at that guy!
I can't believe that I chased that guy!
I can't believe that I chased that guy up a tree.
And I really can't believe that I actually BIT
that guy!

But most of all, I can't believe we were scooped up by Animal Control and sent here! THIS IS ALL MY FAULT! I let my temper get the better of me, and now we're trapped in here!

You see . . . um . . . sometimes
I have trouble controlling my temper.

Do you know anyone like that?

Don't you worry about a thing, handsome. I got us into this mess. I'll figure out a way to get us out . . . somehow. I promise.
GET OUT?!
Why in tarnation would you want to "GET OUT"?

I don't know. Maybe because it's dark and cold and full of weirdos like you.
AHHH . . . You young pups don't know how good you have it!

Don't you worry, son. You're safe here in the county dog shelter. You get two square meals a day and all the water you can drink. There's a rubber ball around here somewhere to play with, though I ain't seen it in about a year now. And every now and then, an actual beam of sunlight comes through that tiny window up there with the bars. There's nothin' out there in the outside world that can be better than THAT!

I should know! I'm **Gramps!** My name is Gramps! But you can call me Gramps. And I've been in here since I was a puppy.

Come to think of it, Gramps is a mighty odd name for a puppy.

But eventually I grew into it. Gramps. I'm Gramps. My name is Gramps.

DON'T LISTEN TO HIM!
HE'S INSANE!

He's old! He's been here too long! He's been institutionalized and doesn't remember what freedom tastes like any more. BUT I DO!

I DO!
Think I'll go find that ball.

Freedom tastes like a hot dog that's rolled off the table and under the sofa and now no one wants it because it's all covered in lint and dust. No one, that is, BUT THE DOG!

Freedom tastes like that delicious slice of ham you snatch up when the baby dips it in applesauce and throws it on the floor because the baby just doesn't appreciate fine cuisine.

Freedom tastes like that big, fat mound of tuna fish that's just sitting there all by itself on the counter, and no one is eating it even though it pleads to you, "Eat me, I beg of you, eat me!" So, the only humane thing to do is to jump up there and eat the tuna fish to put it out of its misery because no one else will do it!

I WANT MY TUNA! I WANT MY HAM! I WANT MY LINT-ENCRUSTED HOT DOG! I WANT MY DELICIOUS, DELICIOUS FREEDOM! AND I SHALL HAVE MY FREEDOM, FOR I AM **HERCULES** AND I HAVE A FOOLPROOF PLAN FOR ESCAPE!

HERCULES' FOOLPROOF
① COLLECT NAIL CLIPPINGS FROM DOGS.
② PLACE NAIL CLIPPINGS INTO WAFFLE IRON.
③ REMOVE DELICIOUS-LOOKING (BUT PROBABLY INEDIBLE) WAFFLE MADE OUT OF FUSED DOG NAILS.
④ HOLD WAFFLE IN FRONT OF DOGS - CAUSING THEM TO DROOL.

PLAN FOR ESCAPE #591
⑤ COLLECT DROOL IN BOWL.
⑥ HEAT BOWL ON PORTABLE STOVE UNTIL DROOL BOILS.
⑦ CLOUD OF STEAM WILL ALERT GUARD.
?
⑧ WHEN GUARD ENTERS CAGE TO INVESTIGATE, DOGS SNEAK AWAY UNSEEN IN DROOL STEAM.
⑨ FREEDOM!

Interesting.
Interesting.

So, where did you find the waffle iron?

Ummm . . . Hello?

YEAAAAAARGH!!
THERE IS NO WAFFLE IRON!
I HAVE NO WAFFLE IRON!

The plan is useless without a waffle iron!
You have to help me find a waffle iron!

There has to be a waffle iron in here somewhere! Why is there never a waffle iron around when you really need one! All I need is ONE LOUSY STINKIN' WAFFLE IRON!

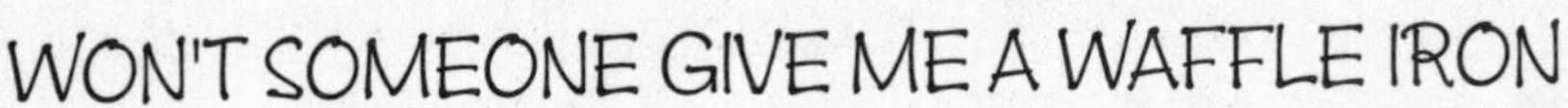
WON'T SOMEONE GIVE ME A WAFFLE IRON

PLEEEASE!!
I'm glad I didn't mention the portable stove.
What was I looking for again?

Hey there, young fella! Why so glum? You're young. You're good lookin'. I'd say that you stand a pretty good chance of getting adopted and going home with a nice family.

The rest of us . . . well . . . that's a different story.

Maybe it isn't fair, but folks tend not to adopt the weird ones.
This NEW plan will work! It HAS to. It's *even* more foolproof than my last plan!

Or the ugly ones—no offense, Miss.
SCRATCH SCRATCH
None taken.

Or the old ones like me. We're here to stay, but you . . . YOU just might get out of here someday.

AND THAT DAY IS TODAY! Thanks to my newest foolproof escape plan, nothing will get in our way of freedom now!
Here we go again.

HERCULES' FOOLPROOF

① COLLECT FLEAS FROM DOGS.

② TRAIN FLEAS TO ATTRACT BIRDS.

③ COLLECT FEATHERS FROM BIRDS.

④ COLLECT FUR FROM DOGS.

PLAN FOR ESCAPE #592

5. PLACE FUR INTO MACHINE THAT TURNS DOG HAIR INTO CHEESE.

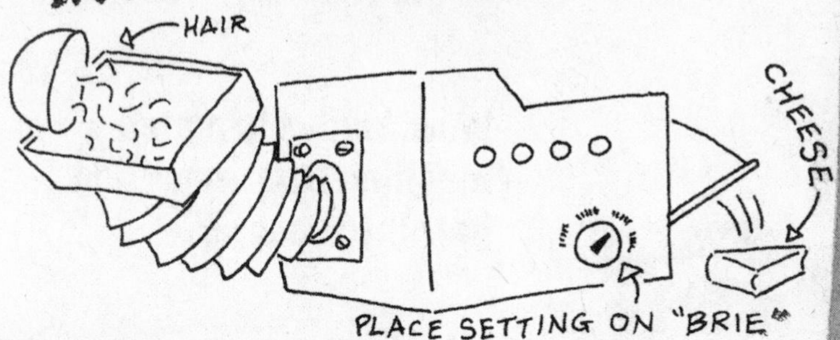

6. USE CHEESE TO APPLY FEATHERS TO DOGS.

7. FREEDOM!

Wow. You've invented a machine that turns dog hair into cheese?

I forgot to invent an ULTRA TRANSFOLIC PASTEURIZER!!! How will I make the cheese?! I have dog hair! But I don't have the cheese! I need the cheese! CHEEEEESE!

Still feeling kind of low, eh, young fella? I hope you know it isn't your fault that you're here. It's never the dog's fault.

My owners had to move away to a place that didn't allow dogs. So they put me here.

My owners had a baby who was allergic to me. So they put me here.

It didn't help that I kept stealing food.

I ran away from my owners. They were not very good dog owners. They treated me very badly, so I ran away. I lived in the dog park up until today.
I don't like to talk about it.

But this guy—THIS GUY—He HAS an owner! I saw him! I even tried to bite him!

I'll bet he's looking for you RIGHT NOW!

Nobody who winds up in here has an owner, Petunia.
That's a fact.

But . . . But . . . That's not true! I saw him! He was real. He was . . .

That big, goofy-looking guy I chased—he was your owner, right?

No?

Told ya.
I'm sorry.
I guess you're officially one of us now.

WAIT . . .
Then who WAS that guy?!

IT'S ME!
UNCLE MURRAY!

You've got a little microchip just under your skin in the back of your neck that told the shelter who you are and where you live! I bet you didn't even know it was there!

I think I can take you home right now. Let me just clear it with that guy who volunteers here.
Farewell, handsome!
Good luck, youngster!
Hasta la juego!

It's him, all right! What a relief! I thought for sure I'd lost the little guy. Can we go home now?
Yup. Just fill out a few forms and you can both go.
Paperwork. There's always paperwork.

Holy salami, was I relieved when we got the call from this guy that you were safe here at the shelter, pooch!
Fare thee well, handsome! Fare thee well!
The name's Strange Kitty.
S.K. for short.

And it looks like they took pretty good care of you! Am I right?
I'll miss you!
Just doing my job, citizen.
Don't forget to initial.

Please think of me sometimes!
Yessiree! Soon I'll get you outta here, and you'll be in your warm, cozy home, in your warm, cozy bed, with your warm, cozy pillow!
Sounds cozy.
Cozy. Cozy. Cozy.

Remember the good times!
Hey! I'll bet even that goofy cat will be happy to see you!
Well, that's everything!
You're free to go!

Okey dokey, pooch! Let's make like bananas and split! AWWW! I guess you're going to miss your little dog park pal, eh? Well, we can always come back to visit.
Only the lonely Know the way I feel tonight . . .
Maybe not.
WHINE
WHINE
WHINE

Huh? What do you mean by "maybe not"?
I mean, she may not be here much longer.

Why?
Well, the report on her says that she bit some guy and chased him up a tree. That's pretty serious. She's been labeled as "aggressive" and a "threat to the community."

WAITAMINNIT! I'M THAT GUY SHE CHASED AND BIT! BUT I'M NOT PRESSING CHARGES! IT'S OKAY! I'M JUST FINE!
It's not that simple. She may have to go.

BUT I'M . . . wait . . . where do dogs like her "go"?
Well . . .

What's . . . what's going to happen to her?
The worst thing you can imagine.

You mean . . .
Yes.

Nobody knows the trouble I've seen . . .
Holy salami!

BUT THAT'S HORRIBLE!!!
Yes, it is.

Something's gotta be done about this!
There's something YOU can do.

Me? What can I do?
Think about it.

Yeah. You're right.

You wait right here, pooch. I gotta go have a conversation.
I was in the bathroom. What did I miss?

What does this guy want?

Easy there, girl. Easy now. Nobody's going to hurt you.
GRRRRRRR

No biting or chomping please. No chasing or scratching, okay? I just want to talk to you.
RRRRR

Hi, dog.

I don't think you like me very much. And you probably trust me even less. But that's because you don't know me. See, I'm a nice guy. Really. I don't smoke. I don't gamble. I don't curse . . . well . . . not that often. I have friends. I have a wife who loves me. I have a nice car. I have a nice house with a big backyard. I have a TV with more channels than I can count. I have a lawn mower. I have a refrigerator. I have a blender. I have a machine that can make coffee almost all by itself.

It's kind of incredible, really, when you think about it. All I have to do every morning is pour in a little coffee, pour in a little water, push a button, and five minutes later I have some pretty good coffee. Of course, I have to add in the milk and sugar myself, but . . .

Sorry. I kind of lost track there. What was my point? RIGHT. My point is this—I have lots and lots of stuff. Honestly, I didn't even mention most of the stuff I have.
But the one thing I don't have . . .

I don't have a dog.

So what do you say, girl? You wanna come home with me? You wanna be my dog?

We can . . . you know . . . if you like the idea . . . shake a paw to make it official.

LICK

IT'S OFFICIAL!
I, UNCLE MURRAY, AM NOW A DOG OWNER!
I've never been so happy.

Yo, Gramps! I have another foolproof plan for escape! But we don't have much time!

All we have to do is make with the sad, desperate googly eyes! It never fails!

C'mon, Gramps! Make with the googly eyes!
I am!

AND THEM, TOO! THEM, TOO! ALL DOGS GO HOME WITH ME!!!
IT WORKED! It actually worked! I'm a genius!

WOWEE! What a day this has turned into!
You are a true gentleman. Let me just finish this paperwork, and you're all free to go.
Paperwork. Always paperwork.
Never did find that ball.

And don't you forget this!
You came in here with it.

All right, pooches!
LET'S ALL GO
HOME!

Thanks for everything!
My pleasure.
Vaya con Dios!

Say, what are you anyway?
Who, me? I'm a volunteer here at the dog shelter.

No. I mean . . . what ARE you?
Oh, I see. I am a proud member of the sphynx breed of hairless cats.

Really?! You're a cat? Neat. I thought you were maybe some kind of shaved llama or something.
Well, goodbye!

Shaved llama. That would be cool.
Totally cool.

KITTY'S HORRIBLE
BUT TRUE FACTS ABOUT
DOGS

Why Do Dogs Lick Faces?

Cats rarely lick faces, but when they do it's for the same reasons they lick themselves or other cats: to groom you or taste something that might be interesting. Dogs, however, are different. Very different.

GROSS
DO NOT
TOUCH
KEEP
AWAY

Dogs lick people because they're hoping to eat any regurgitated food you might have on your face. THAT'S RIGHT! YOU READ THAT RIGHT! DON'T TURN AWAY! FACE THE UGLY TRUTH! Dogs want to eat your throw up!

Say a wild dog, like a wolf mother, kills a deer. Rather than try to drag her prey all the way back to her den, she'll eat as much as she can and then carry her food back inside her stomach. Her puppies will then lick her face to make her regurgitate her food for them to eat. And if this notion doesn't make you want to regurgitate your own breakfast, then I don't know what else will.

This means that when a dog or a puppy licks YOUR face, he's following the same instinct he used when he wanted his mother to vomit on him. I REPEAT . . . Puppies WANT their mothers to vomit on them.

CARTOON BY KITTY

Oh sure, dogs will lick people's faces for other reasons. They like the taste of your salty sweat and tears. They might like the taste of that new skin lotion you're using.

And, of course, dogs like to lick people as a sign of affection or excitement or happiness. Dogs sometimes lick people's faces as a sign of submission just as they once did with their own mothers. Licking is a signal they give to people that they're comfortable around you.

But regardless of the reasons, licking people is gross. Dogs are gross. And licking people is just another item in a long list of disgusting dog habits.

So if there are any cats out there reading this who actually lick people—that is a sick dog thing. SO CUT IT OUT!

*If you LICK, you are SICK!

• PART FOUR •

PUPPY LOYALTY

Gang, there's a goofy cat in there that's capable of anything. So I'm sending Puppy here inside, and then we're all going home.
See you around, handsome!

Okey dokey, pooches! That's done, so let's all go . . .

HEY, YOU!

Officer, PLEASE! I just want to bring my dogs home! They all have leashes I bought at the shelter. They all have licenses. I have loads of plastic bags. And my belt is on nice and tight. It's been a long day, and we all just want to go home!

I JUST WANTED TO TELL YOU—THAT'S A GREAT LOOKIN' BUNCH OF DOGS YA GOT THERE! I LOVE DOGS! YOU TAKE GOOD CARE OF THEM, OKAY?

You bet,
officer.

I'm going to give them the best home they ever had!

MEANWHILE . . .

WELCOME HOME, PUPPY! Boy, we're glad to have you back safe and sound. But we have to warn you—Kitty is still just as ornery and cross as ever, and we still can't figure out why.

I've been busy digging an underground bunker in the backyard where we can all live from now on.

Puppy, did you hear me? Approaching Kitty right now is probably a terrible idea.

PLOP!

Puppy! You found Mousey-mouse! I haven't seen Mousey-mouse since yesterday.

Wait a minute . . .
YAWN

All this mayhem—all this chaos—all of this wanton carnage and destruction—this is all because Mousey-mouse was missing?
ARE YOU KIDDING ME?!

KITTY, IS THIS WHY YOU'VE BEEN IN SUCH A FOUL, WRETCHED MOOD ALL DAY? IS THIS WHY WE'VE BEEN LIVING IN CONSTANT TERROR ALL THIS TIME? IS THIS WHY THE PIANO IS ON THE ROOF AND THE CAR IS IN THE BASEMENT? IS THIS WHY OUR NEIGHBORS HAVE CHANGED THEIR NAMES AND MOVED OUT OF THE COUNTRY? ALL THIS—ALL THIS BECAUSE YOU COULDN'T FIND MOUSEY-MOUSE FOR ONE STINKING DAY?! IS THIS SOME KIND OF SICK JOKE? KITTY! KITTY! DON'T YOU DARE IGNORE ME. KITTY THIS IS SERIOUS! KITTY, I KNOW YOU CAN HEAR ME! KITTY, WE HAVE TO HAVE A VERY SERIOU... LL THIS!

• APPENDIX ONE •

MEET THE BREEDS

Petunia • Bulldog

Despite its stern and formidable appearance, the bulldog is a very loving and gentle pet. But they did once have a very savage side to their personality when they were first bred to leap up and bite a bull's nose with their powerful jaws just before bullfights. But this ferocious past is long behind them.

Hercules • Chihuahua

Though considered the smallest dogs in the world and weighing as little as only 2 pounds, chihuahuas can have a fierce and dominating personality. Archaeologists have discovered the remains of these dogs inside of Mayan tombs, because people believed them to be so sacred that they could guide them in the afterlife.

Gramps • Lhasa Apso

The history of these dogs goes back more than 1,300 years to when they were guard dogs in Tibetan monasteries. Though their eyesight is compromised by the long hair that covers their faces, their hearing is exceptionally good. As you can imagine, that luxurious coat of theirs requires daily brushing to stay that way.

Puppy • Mutt

Any dog whose breed cannot be recognized, usually because it's a blend of two or more breeds, is commonly known as a "mutt" or "mongrel." These dogs are just as loving and fun as any purebred. In fact, studies have shown that mutts tend to be healthier and live longer than their purebred cousins.

• APPENDIX TWO •

PET ADOPTION

There are an estimated 6 MILLION to 8 MILLION dogs and cats living in pet shelters in the United States. Only about 25 percent of them are ever adopted. Although these shelters do their absolute best to keep their animals healthy and safe, the reality is that they are all overcrowded.

For information on how you can help animals living in shelters go to . . .

humanesociety.org
or
aspca.org

For information on how you can find the right pet for you to adopt from a shelter go to . . .

adoptapet.com
or
petfinder.com

More BAD KITTY Madness!

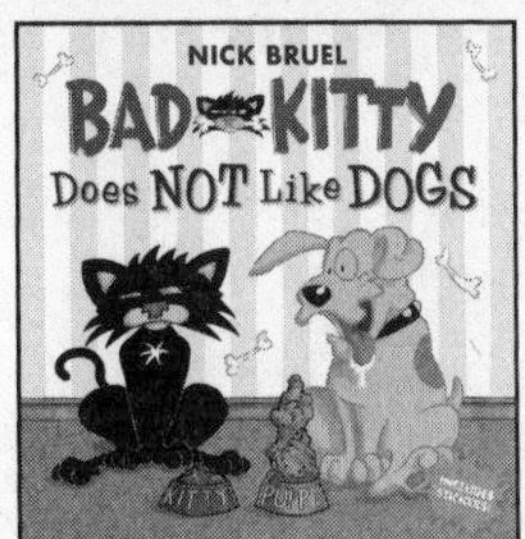

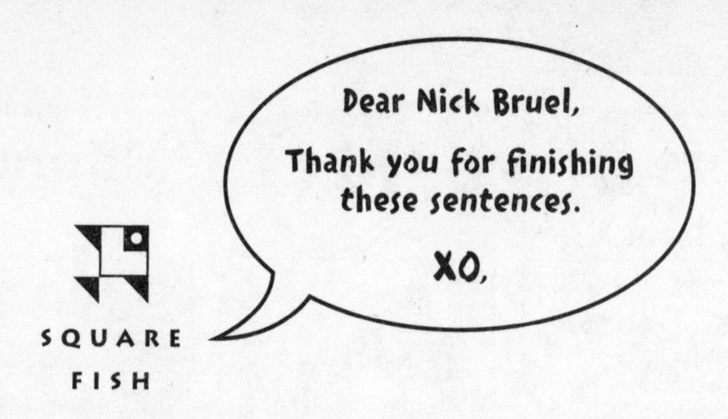

Dear Nick Bruel,
Thank you for finishing these sentences.
XO,
SQUARE FISH

If I were a puppy . . .

then I would do everything in my power to enjoy being a puppy. I was a puppy once. I used to frolic outside and run around the house and roll in dirt without a care in the world. I used to play with such enthusiasm that I thought I would never tire out. But then I grew up and became a big, tired, old dog. And now that I am an old dog, I have come to realize that I never really appreciated how wonderful it was to be a puppy. And now, of course, I miss it. Being an old dog isn't that bad. But being a puppy was better.

I always . . .

read to my puppy every night. Our daughter Izzy can't fall asleep without having at least two books read to her every night. And in case anyone is wondering, her favorite books are NOT Bad Kitty books. She loves books by Ezra Jack Keats and Cynthia Rylant and Arnold Lobel. So do I.

I wish I could . . .

play the piano and speak Chinese. These, of course, were the two things my mother wanted me to do the most, but I was very resistant when I was a puppy. And now I regret it. I am comforted, however, by the notion that it's never too late. The only question, though, is whether or not an old dog can learn new tricks.

Puppy should . . .

do whatever he can to make that cat play with him. He will always fail, but he should never give up.

Puppy loves . . .

to play. PLAY! PLAY! PLAY!

Kitty loves . . .

to sleep. SLEEP! SLEEP! SLEEP! This is one reason why Kitty and Puppy have trouble finding common ground.

When I'm in a *bad* mood . . .

I try to take a shower. Long, hot showers clear my head better than anything else. Not coincidentally, perhaps, a long shower is also often the source of great creative inspiration for me.

***Look!* It's a . . .**

massive, powdery white ice crystal beast floating in the sky! **Where?!** There! **Where?!** Right in front of you! **Where?!** Right there above us! **You mean that thing?!** It's about to drop on us and crush us all like a bowling ball rolling over an anthill! **You mean that?!** YES, THAT! **That's a cloud.** A what? **A cloud.** Oh . . . then maybe we should get an umbrella.

But why didn't you ask me about . . .

my recipe for baked salmon? Mix together 1/4 cup of lemon and/or lime juice with 1/4 cup of olive oil and two finely chopped cloves of garlic. Pour the mixture over a large filet of salmon lying skin side down on aluminum foil. Wrap the foil loosely around the fish and seal up the top. Marinate the fish in the refrigerator for an hour or longer. Bake at 375 degrees Fahrenheit for about 30 minutes. Delicious.

Editor's note: Kids, remember not to use the oven yourself! If you want some salmon, give this recipe to a responsible adult.

It's time for this sick kitty to go to the vet!

Keep reading for a sneak peek of

Bad Kitty Goes to the Vet.

•CHAPTER ONE•

POOR, SICK KITTY

This is what Kitty looks like when she's a happy, healthy pussycat.

She has lots of energy.

She has a good appetite.

She has a really, REALLY good appetite.

And she keeps herself nice and clean.

But that's not how Kitty looks today. She looks terrible. She looks tired. She looks unhappy. She does not look healthy at all.

And worst of all . . . Kitty is just not eating her food.

Kitty, I don't understand why you're not eating. I've watched grown men cry trying to beat you at a hot dog eating contest. I once saw you swallow an entire liver and pineapple pizza in one gulp. I've seen you consume an entire meatloaf the size of a car in just five minutes. It was horrifying.

This is the warning poster that hangs over the meat counter of every grocery store in the county.

HAIR: Black
EYES: Yellow
HEIGHT: 11"
WEIGHT: 8.5 lbs.

This hungry feline felon has been known to distract innocent butchers with soulful eyes and a sequence of sad meows until she suddenly devours all stock in a matter of minutes.

Do not attempt to engage. Feline is heavily armed with claws, sharp teeth, and projectile hair balls.

Call police, animal control, and air force if nasty, violent feline is sighted.

But today you're not even touching your breakfast! Please, Kitty! Eat something! You're starting to get us worried.

Try to sit up, Kitty. Let's check you out. Maybe you have a hair ball caught in your throat.

Nothing? Hmmmm . . . I think I should feel your belly just to see if you have any lumps.

Hold still, Kitty. I promise this won't hurt one bit.

HEE-YUK! BWAH-HEE-
HAR-HAR-HA! HO-HEE-
HO-HAR-HEE-HAR-HA!

Sorry about that, Kitty. I honestly had no idea you were so ticklish.